P9-CJH-654

Dream Dancer

STORY BY JILL NEWSOME

ILLUSTRATIONS BY CLAUDIO MUÑOZ

HarperCollinsPublishers

To our own Lily Fernanda

Dream Dancer
Text copyright © 2001 by Jill Newsome
Illustrations copyright © 2001 by Claudio Muñoz
Printed in Italy. All rights reserved.
www.harperchildrens.com

Library of Congress Cataloging-in-Publication Data
is available.
ISBN 0-06-000932-2 — ISBN 0-06-001322-2 (lib. bdg.)

1 2 3 4 5 6 7 8 9 10

First HarperCollins Edition, 2002
Originally published in Great Britain
by Andersen Press Ltd., 2001

Lily loved to dance.

She danced in the morning.

She danced in the evening.

She danced all around the house

and on her way to school,

come rain or shine,
and even in the sea.

Whether at the dance class
or rehearsing for the Show,

they said she danced like a dream.

The fact is that Lily also danced in her dreams.

But the dream turned into a nightmare
the day she had a bad fall,
the day she had to stop
and forget all about her lessons
and all about the Show.

Day followed after day
and week followed after week.
Sad little Lily,
like a fish out of water,
like a cheetah in a cage.

But one sunny afternoon
Grandma took Lily to tea
and in the window of the toy shop
a little dancer appeared.

Every time they walked by
she seemed to be in a different pose.

What a special surprise when Grandma
gave Lily that little dancing doll.
Lily called her Peggy . . .

. . . and from that day they were never seen apart.

Peggy loved to dance.

She danced in the morning,

she danced in the evening,

she danced on their way to school

and even in the bath!

Whatever they did,

wherever they went,
Peggy just couldn't help dancing.

But where she danced her best
was in Lily's Magic Show.

And so, after days and days
and weeks and months and nearly a year,
the moment came at last
when Lily could dance again.

Then a dark thought froze her stiff:
what if she had forgotten how to dance?
She needed Peggy, but where was she?

There she was, already joining in the class!

So Lily did too.

And though it happened
little by little,

and it took days . . .

. . . and weeks . . .

. . . and months,

Lily danced once more like a dream.
And in her special way . . .

. . . Peggy did too.